April Fool!

VIKING
Published by the Penguin Group
Penguin Putnam Books for Young Readers, 345 Hudson Street, New York, New York
10014, U.S.A.
Penguin Books Ltd, 27 Wrights Lane, London W8 5TZ, England
Penguin Books Australia Ltd, Ringwood, Victoria, Australia
Penguin Books Canada Ltd, 10 Alcorn Avenue, Toronto, Ontario, Canada M4V 3B2
Penguin Books (N.Z.) Ltd, 182-190 Wairau Road, Auckland 10, New Zealand

Penguin Books Ltd, Registered Offices: Harmondsworth, Middlesex, England

First published in 2000 by Viking and Puffin Books, divisions of Penguin Putnam
Books for Young Readers

3 5 7 9 10 8 6 4 2

LIBRARY OF CONGRESS CATALOGING-IN-PUBLICATION DATA:
April Fool! / by Harriet Ziefert; illustrated by Chris Demarest
p. cm. — (A Viking easy-to-read)
Summary: On April 1, Will tells his friends how he once saw a bike-
riding elephant who sang through his trunk while juggling six bags
of junk.
ISBN 0-670-88762-5 (hardcover). ISBN 0-14-130582-7 (pbk).
[1. April Fool's Day Fiction. 2. Elephants Fiction. 3. Stories in rhyme.]
I. Demarest, Chris L., ill. II. Title. III. Series.
PZ8.3.Z47Ap 2000 [E]—dc21 99-26014 CIP

Viking® and Easy-to-Read® are registered trademarks of Penguin Putnam Inc.

Reading level 1.8

Printed in Hong Kong

APRIL FOOL!

A Viking Easy-to-Read

by Harriet Ziefert
illustrated by Chris Demarest

VIKING

"Today is April first, you know,"
said Will to Sam and Cory.

"Walk along to school with me,
and I'll tell you a story."

"I once saw an elephant,
going to school.

He had on a hat.
It looked very cool."

"His trunk was big.
His tail was not.

His eye was little—
a tiny black dot."

"He raced with a bus
that was going to town.

He put back a flagpole
that had fallen down."

"His back was long.
His back was wide.

He picked up five kids
and gave them a ride."

"He lifted his legs.
He did some tricks.

He scared the kids
with his elephant kicks."

"He stood on one leg and
sang through his trunk.

He started to juggle
six bags full of junk."

"He opened his back pack.
Inside was his lunch.

He gave all the kids . . .

some peanuts to munch."

"He packed up his back pack
and waved good-bye.

'Don't go! Don't go!'
I heard the kids cry."